THIS BOOK BELONGS TO

To Jessica. My best friend, my partner, my everything.

With special thanks to Merideth Harte and Cindy Loh.

STERLING CHILDREN'S BOOKS
New York
An Imprint of Sterling Publishing
387 Park Avenue South
New York, NY 10016

ISBN 978-1-4027-8830-7 (hardcover)

Distributed in Canada by Sterling Publishing
c/o Canadian Manda Group, 165 Dufferin Street
Toronto, Ontario, Canada M6K 3H6
Distributed in the United Kingdom by GMC Distribution Services
Castle Place, 166 High Street, Lewes, East Sussex, England BN7 1XU
Distributed in Australia by Capricorn Link (Australia) Pty. Ltd.
P.O. Box 704, Windsor, NSW 2756, Australia

For information about custom editions, special sales, and premium and corporate purchases, please contact Sterling Special Sales at 800-805-5489 or specialsales@sterlingpublishing.com.

Printed in China

Lot #:
2 4 6 8 10 9 7 5 3 1
02/12

www.sterlingpublishing.com/kids

# SAD
# SANTA

## TAD CARPENTER

**DECEMBER 26TH WAS A BEAUTIFUL DAY.**

The birds were singing. The air was crisp.

Children all over the world were playing

with their new toys and presents.

But, for Santa, **DECEMBER 26TH** was a horrible,
awful day. It was the **WORST DAY OF THE YEAR.**

There were no toys to make, no cookies to eat, and no presents to wrap. Christmas was over, and **SANTA WAS SAD**.

"**CHEER UP, SANTA**," said the elves. "This was the best Christmas of them all! The gifts were delivered on time. The stockings were filled by the chimney with care. You checked your list twice. And you didn't even get a speck of soot on your coat."

Santa tried to be merry, but after Christmas the candy canes looked **LESS MINTY**, the decorations seemed **LESS TWINKLY**, and even Santa's hat was **LESS SNUGGLY**.

When the sleigh team heard about **SAD SANTA**, they stopped playing reindeer games and tried to make him **JOLLY AGAIN**.

"Look on the bright side, Santa. We beat last year's record: **196 COUNTRIES IN 8 HOURS** and we didn't look at the map once."

Even though that was all true, **SANTA WAS STILL SAD**.

Nothing would **LIFT SANTA'S SPIRITS**. Christmas was over and already **FORGOTTEN**. Everyone was busy, busy, busy, gearing up for New Year's.

REINDEER TREATS
COOKIE RECIPES
SLEIGH FLYING

It was time to call in the boss.

"Maybe you need a vacation," suggested Mrs. Claus. "Why don't you **TAKE A BREAK** and we can get away from it all? That will get your mind off of things. Remember: **NEXT CHRISTMAS IS ONLY 364 DAYS AWAY** and Christmas won't be Christmas with a sad Santa."

Santa was **STILL SAD**, but they loaded up the sleigh and went to the **BEACH** anyway.

Sad Santa **TRIED TO RELAX**. But the sand kept
getting stuck in his boots. The sun was **TOO HOT**
and made his whiskers itchy. The pineapple
coconut slushee just wasn't the same as a warm
cup of cocoa.

**SANTA MISSED** his workshop. He missed Mrs. Claus's gingersnap **COOKIES**. He missed the frosty icicles at the North Pole. He missed the **HAPPY CHILDREN** who looked forward to his annual visit. But Christmas was over. Nobody needed Santa anymore.

Just when all hope was lost, when sad Santa was sure that he would never feel merry again, a little bit of **CHRISTMAS MAGIC** came his way.

NORTH POLE SHIPPING

317 West Jolly St.
North Pole, NP
102003

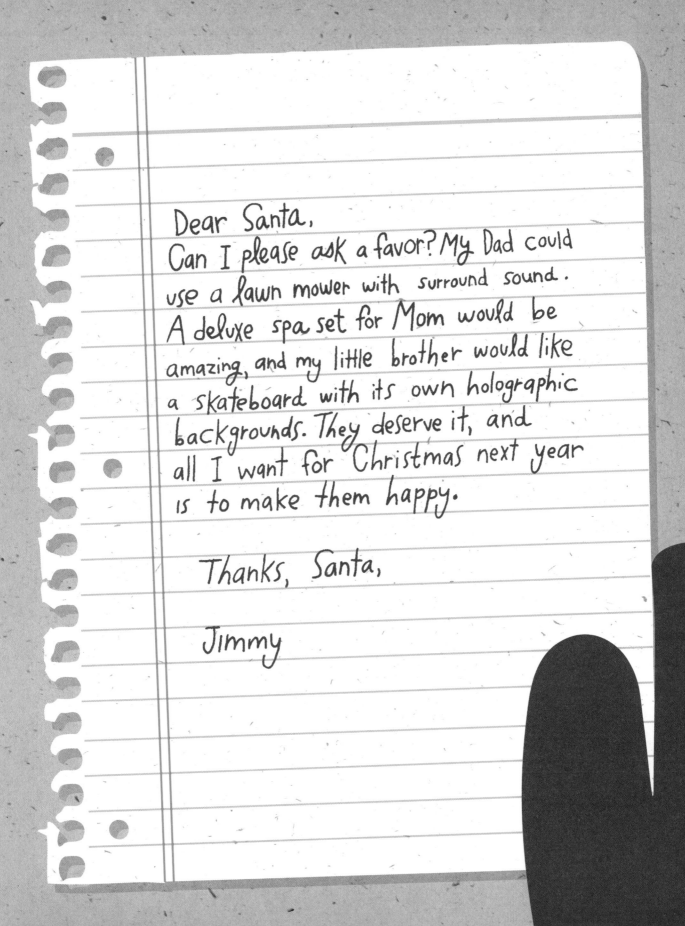

Dear Santa,
Can I please ask a favor? My Dad could
use a lawn mower with surround sound.
A deluxe spa set for Mom would be
amazing, and my little brother would like
a skateboard with its own holographic
backgrounds. They deserve it, and
all I want for Christmas next year
is to make them happy.

Thanks, Santa,

Jimmy

"What's this about?" Santa asked. "Surround
sound lawn mower?

"Deluxe spa set? A skateboard with a holographic
projection screen? All for his family?"

"This boy **NEEDS** me!" sad Santa realized. "**ALL THE CHILDREN AND FAMILIES AROUND THE WORLD NEED ME!**"

**THERE WAS NO TIME TO LOSE.** Santa rushed back to the North Pole and got to work right away. He didn't want to let anybody down. Even if he couldn't deliver exactly what was asked for, sad Santa was **DETERMINED** to make sure everyone got something **EXTRA-SPECIAL** next Christmas.

FLAT SCREEN

WINGS TO TAKE
FLIGHT

3-D
GLASSES

HIGH DEF

3-D

BOX
1297
CHANNELS
& EVERY
GAME SYSTEM

MODEL #: 122511022581062182

SUPER SONIC
EXTREME SKATE
BOARD

Santa sat in his **BEST THINKING CHAIR**. He sharpened all his #2 pencils and started to design **SOMETHING WONDERFUL**.

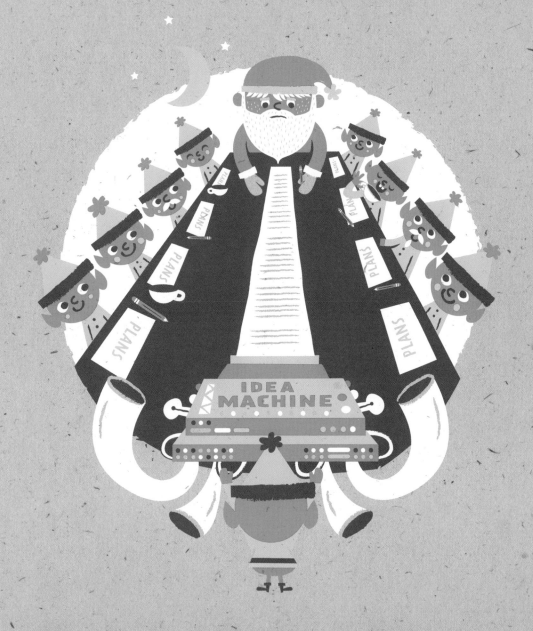

He called a meeting with his top tech team. They worked all day and all night.

And with every blueprint and every new idea,
sad Santa started to get his **PEP** back in his step,
his **HO** back in his ho-ho-ho, and a **JINGLE** back
in his bells.

Sad Santa felt like his old holly, **JOLLY SELF**
again, because he remembered one very
important thing: The **SPIRIT OF THE SEASON**
is about giving, caring, and living as if it were
Christmas every single day of the year.

**361 : 11 : 14 : 26**

DAYS      MONTHS      HOURS      MINUTES

From that day on,
**SANTA WAS NEVER SAD AGAIN.**